The Rugrats Versus the Monkeys

by Luke David

illustrated by John Kurtz and Sandrina Kurtz

Simon Spotlight/Nickelodeon

Rugrats created by Arlene Klasky, Gabor Csupo, and Paul Germain

SIMON SPOTLIGHT
An imprint of Simon & Schuster Children's Publishing Division
1230 Avenue of the Americas
New York, New York 10020

Manufactured in the United States of America

First Edition   10 9 8 7 6 5 4 3

ISBN 0-689-82142-5

The circus was coming to town! *Choo-choo-chugchug! Choo-choo-chugchug!* The circus train rushed through the countryside.

Rattle! Bang! Smash! The train cars jumped off the tracks and rolled into the forest. Uh-oh! The circus monkeys escaped from their cages.

Meanwhile at the Pickleses' house, Tommy and his new baby brother Dil went for a ride in the Reptar wagon that their father had invented. The brothers were joined by Tommy's friends Chuckie, Phil, and Lil.

First the babies drove the wagon through a lemonade stand, and then they took a ride in the back of a mattress truck.

Finally, after journeying some ways into the woods, the babies came to a full stop.

"Where are we?" asked Phil.

"I dunno, but let's figure out how to get home," said Tommy.

Suddenly Chuckie started stammering, "C–C–C–Clowns!" He pointed at a huge painted clown.

The babies discovered that the clown was a picture that had been painted on a train. The train was lying in a jumble on the forest floor.

Suddenly Phil spotted a little monkey cranking an old music box. "Wow, you never know what you're gonna find in the forest, do you?" said Phil.

Soon the babies were surrounded by a large number of monkeys. The monkeys began to play with the babies.

"Hungry, hungry!" Dil started wailing.

Tommy loved playing with the monkeys, but he stopped so he could feed his baby brother. He opened a jar of banana baby food and accidentally spilled some on the diaper bag. One of the monkeys grabbed the bag and ran off.

"Hey, come back here, you monkey!" Tommy yelled after him.

Just then, Chuckie yelled, "Help!"
Kerplunk! He fell out of a tree and landed on Tommy.
"Quit playing around, Chuckie, and watch Dil,"
he said. "I gotta get that diapie bag!"
"Tommy . . . " Chuckie started, but
Tommy had left.

Chuckie noticed a monkey pulling Dil out of the wagon.
"Hey! Leave him alone! He's not a nanner!" Chuckie cried out.
He grabbed Dil from the monkey.

Immediately monkeys started pulling on both Chuckie and Dil.
Phil and Lil grabbed Dil.

Then one of the monkeys swiped Chuckie's glasses. "Let go! Let
go!" Chuckie yelled.

At that moment Phil and Lil let go of Dil, and the monkeys
dragged him away.

"Oh, this is just great!" said Chuckie. "I tell ya it can't get any worser than—"

Crunch! Chuckie stepped on his glasses. He put them on his nose. It was hard to see now because the lenses were cracked.

"Well, at least the monkeys are gone," Phil said.

"Yeah, and they tooked baby Dil with them," added Lil.

"But Tommy told me to watch him! This is bad, bad, bad!" Chuckie wailed.

"Well, maybe Tommy never has to know," said Phil. "Look!" He wrapped a baby monkey in a blanket so it looked like Dil.

Tommy came back with the diaper bag. He looked in the wagon. "Hey! That's not my brother!" he said.

"Well, we thought you wouldn't mind having a monkey for a brother. You know, instead of Dil," said Chuckie slowly.

"Yeah, Dil isn't any fun," said Phil.

"But he's my brother. I gotta find him!" said Tommy. "C'mon, Chuckie, I need your help. You're my bestest friend!"

"If I'm your bestest friend, then how come you didn't help me when I was in trouble?" said Chuckie. "Sorry, Tommy, I'm going with Phil and Lil. We're going to find a way back home."

"Well, fine," Tommy said, sadly. "I'll go get Dil from the monkeys by myself." He turned and went into the woods.

It had started to rain.

Tommy followed the sound of his brother's crying. When he caught up with Dil, he found him being carried away by two monkeys.

"Hey! Gimme back my brother!" Tommy yelled. "Get out of here, you monkeys!"

Startled, the monkeys let go of Dil and ran away.

"We'll just have a little bottle and take a nice nappie. Everything will be okay," Tommy said to Dil as he carried him to a tree hollow to get out of the rain. Tommy took out a bottle of milk and a blanket.

"Mine!" yelled Dil, grabbing both.

"That's it! Phil and Lil were right!" Tommy said angrily. "You're a naughty bad baby! I'm through being your big brother!"

Lightning flashed and thunder boomed. Terrified, Dil wrapped himself around Tommy. Tommy hugged him tight.

"I'm sorry, Dil," said Tommy. "Everything's going to be okay." Dil looked up at Tommy. Then his head flopped onto Tommy's chest, and he fell asleep. Tommy smiled down at his sleeping brother.

Meanwhile Chuckie followed Phil and Lil down a path into another part of the woods. Thunder boomed. Lightning flashed. *Cra-a-a-ck!* A tree nearly came down on top of them.

"Aaaargh!" they cried out.

Chuckie was okay. Lil was okay. But the only thing they could find of Phil were his shoes.

"He always loved climbing on trees," said Chuckie. "Now a tree's climbed on him!"

"He was my favoritest brother," Lil said. "Speak to me, Phillip!"

"Have you guys seen my shoes?" Phil popped up from the other side of the tree.

"Phillip!" Lil cried. She jumped over the tree and gave him a big hug.

"Phew!" said Chuckie. "Now we gotta make sure Tommy is okay too!"

"No, we don't," said Lil.

Phil agreed with her. "All Tommy cares about now is Baby Dil," he said.

"Oh, come on guys!" said Chuckie.

Meanwhile, Tommy and Dil were surrounded by monkeys. They were drawn by Dil's open jar of banana baby food.

"Not so fast, you monkeys!" said Phil as he and Lil suddenly appeared on the scene.

"Phil! Lil! You came!" shouted Tommy. "But where's . . ."

At that moment everyone turned to see—Chuckie! He was waving a jar of baby food.

"Hey, monkeys!" Chuckie roared. "You want nanners? Well, come and get them!" He started running with the monkeys in hot pursuit.

"Gosh, I never knowed Chuckie was so brave," said Lil.

"Yeah, I'm gonna miss him," said Phil.

"You guys take Dil," said Tommy. "I gotta go help my bestest friend!"

Chuckie ran with all his might, but the monkeys were right
behind him. Suddenly he skidded to a stop. Right in front of him
was the edge of a cliff. He had nowhere to go! He turned and faced
the monkeys.

Just as the monkeys were about to grab him, Tommy arrived riding Spike, who had followed the babies' trail into the forest.

"C'mon, Chuckie!" yelled Tommy. He and Spike burst through the crowd of monkeys and scooped up Chuckie.

"Whoooaaa!" cried out Chuckie.

Meanwhile Phil and Lil jumped into the Reptar wagon with Dil. Soon they were joined by Tommy, Chuckie, and Spike as they ran away from the monkeys. Next Angelica, who had been following the babies ever since Dil took her Cynthia doll, also grabbed on. The wagon started across a bridge.

The monkeys followed the babies onto the bridge, but then ran away, and the Rugrats never saw them again.

Soon after, the Rugrats were rescued by their parents.

All the babies were brought home safe and sound.

And if it hadn't been for Dil, the Rugrats wouldn't have had such an exciting adventure.